Koala and Emu
and the Unexpected Box

by
Esta de Fossard

Photographs by Neil McLeod
Drawings by Lynn Twelftree

The Koala Stories • Series 3

Published by

 Edward Arnold (Australia) Pty. Ltd.

For Gordon and Gotch Limited

One day when Koala was looking at the peaceful world around his favourite tree, he noticed something he had never seen before. An interesting looking box in the branch of a nearby tree.

"Hmmm," said Koala. "That's a most unexpected box. I wonder what it is."

Koala was about to scramble out of his tree and look more closely, when he saw Emu striding up in the direction of the tree.

2

"Hi, Emu," called Koala. "Do you know what that box is all about?"

"Er . . . what . . . um," muttered Emu, who had been startled by the sound of Koala's voice. "What box?"

"THAT box," repeated Koala. "What is it?"

"Oh . . . THAT," said Emu, trying to look as if the box had not been a surprise. "Oh, that belongs to me."

"Oh," said Koala, who was quite sure Emu had not seen the box before, "but what's in it, Emu?"

"Ah . . . er . . . well . . . um," spluttered Emu. "Well now, that's a secret, Koala. It's a very special secret, and it belongs to me."

"Well, then, what's it doing up in a tree?" Koala asked.

"Ah . . . er . . . well . . . um,"
spluttered Emu again. "It's . . . it's up there
for safe keeping. It is such a very special
secret box that I have to keep it in a safe
place all the time."

"But, Emu . . ." Koala went on.

"Really, Koala, you DO ask a lot of
questions," said Emu.

"Sorry," said Koala. "But . . . but . . . I
wanted to ask you . . . emus can't fly, so
how can you reach that box when you want
it?"

"Ah . . . er . . . well . . . um," said
Emu, walking around the tree and looking
up at the box, "ah . . . er . . . well . . .
um, I just stretch myself up very tall, and I
. . . ah . . . er . . . well . . . um, I just
reach it."

"Oh!" said Koala, and he turned around and prepared to take a snooze in the sun.

Now the fact of the matter was indeed that Emu had never seen the box until Koala mentioned it. And Emu was just as curious as Koala about that box. And Emu wanted to find out what was inside it. But how?

Emu marched over to the tree and looked up. Emu reached up. Emu stretched and stretched and stretched up. But it was no use. The box stayed just out of reach.

"Grrr . . . grooblespooks!" spluttered Emu. "Now what am I going to do? I want that box and I mean to get that box. But how am I going to reach it?"

"You need a log to stand on," said Goanna, who had been watching quietly from the comfort of a sunny log near the tree.

"Oh . . . oh . . . yes, good idea," said Emu. "Er, let me borrow your log for a few minutes, Goanna."

"No!" said Goanna. "It's taken me a long time to find this log, and I'm very comfortable here now. I don't feel like moving again . . . unless . . ."

"Unless what?" demanded Emu.

"Unless it's really worth it," said Goanna, looking up knowingly at the box in the tree.

"Ah ha," said Emu. "But that's my box, Goanna. It's a very special secret box and everything in it belongs to me."

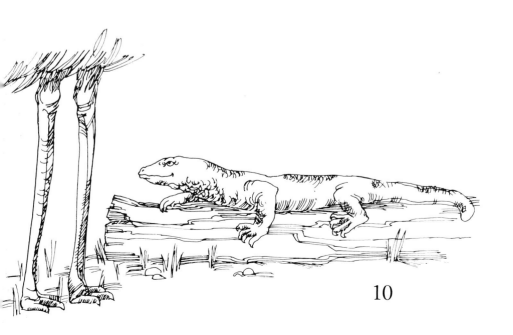

"Oh," said Goanna, "then I guess you're going to have to reach it all by yourself."

Emu looked at Goanna, and then looked at the box again. "Well," said Emu, "I suppose I could share some of it with you, if you help me."

"Half of it!" demanded Goanna, without moving a muscle.

"Half of it!" exploded Emu. "Why, that's . . . that's . . ." But Emu had no other choice, and was forced to give in to Goanna.

But an emu is a lot heavier than a goanna, and when all that emu weight landed on the log, it began to wobble.

"Oooh . . . aaah . . . eeech," screeched Emu. "The log's wobbling, Goanna. How can I ever reach my box with your silly log wobbling around all over the place?"

"Well now, what you're wanting is some way to keep that log steady," said Wombat, from under the bushes.

"I know that," growled Emu, trying to stay upright on the wobbly log. "But how?"

"It's someone to dig a hole around it you need," said Wombat. "That way the log will be being firmly wedged and won't be after wobbling around all over the place."

"Well, dig it then, Wombat," ordered Emu. "You're good at digging, so dig a hole for me."

"I can't be doing that," said Wombat.
"I can't be stopping and digging holes every
time a foolish creature gets stuck on a log
that's wobbling all over the place. I have
better things to do."

"But . . . but . . . Wombat," spluttered
Emu. "You have to help me. I can't reach
my box without help."

"I'm after thinking that isn't my problem,"
said Wombat.

"Well . . . I could . . . I could . . ."
began Emu, "I suppose I could give you part
of what's in the box if you help me."

"I'd be agreeing to take half of it, I would,"
said Wombat.

"But half of it belongs to me," said Goanna.

"Well then, I'll be after needing half of
what belongs to you Goanna, and half of
what belongs to Emu."

Emu and Goanna looked at each other.
They had no other choice.

"Oh, very well," said Emu.

So Wombat got busy digging a hole around the log so that it would be firmly wedged and wouldn't wobble when Emu stood on it to reach the box.

But all that digging didn't seem to do much good.

"There's too much sand," panted Wombat. "Every time I'm after digging the hole, the sand is after falling in and filling it up again."

"It's sticks you need! Sticks you need!" screeched Cockatoo, from overhead. "Put sticks in the hole to stop the sand falling in."

"Indeed and that's a very good idea, it is," said Wombat. "You're the one to be having a good strong beak, Cockatoo, and you're the one to be using sticks for your nest, so I'm after thinking you could be fetching the sticks to make the hole strong."

"Why should I do that?" shrieked Cockatoo. "What's in it for me?"
Wombat was about to say something, when Emu interrupted. "No, no, no," shouted Emu. "I'm not going to share any more. That's my box and what's in it belongs to me."

"Except for the part that belongs to me," snapped Goanna.

"And the part that belongs to me," insisted Wombat.

"And the part that belongs to me," said Cockatoo, "if you want my help."

"But . . . but . . . but," spluttered Emu.

"I only want half," said Cockatoo. "Half of yours, Wombat, and half of Goanna's and half of Emu's."

And Emu and Wombat and Goanna had no other choice. They had to agree. "Oh, all right," said Emu.

And Cockatoo flew away to fetch some sticks to put in the bottom of the hole that Wombat was digging around the log so that it would be firmly wedged and wouldn't wobble when Emu stood on it to reach the box.

But when Cockatoo came flying back, it was clear that there was still a problem.

"This will never do," grumbled Emu. "Cockatoo can only carry one stick at a time. We need lots of sticks."

"What we need is something to carry them in," said Koala, whose snooze had been disturbed by all the noise.

"Yes," screeched Cockatoo. "Something to carry them in. But what can we use?"

"We could use your billycan, Koala," said Goanna. "That would be just the thing for carrying the sticks to put in the bottom of the hole that Wombat is digging around the log so that it will be firmly wedged and won't wobble when Emu stands on it to reach the box."

"But I can't do that," Koala said, "unless I find somewhere to put my gum leaves. My billycan is full of gum leaves and I have nowhere else to put them."

"Well, eat them!" shouted Emu rudely.

"I can't do that!" said Koala, in astonishment. "If I eat all those gum leaves at once, I'll get the most awful tummy ache."

"Who cares about your silly old tummy ache?" said Emu. "I just want to get my box. It's my box and what's in it belongs to me."

"Except for the part that belongs to me," said Goanna.

"And the part that belongs to me," added Wombat.

"And the part that belongs to me," screeched Cockatoo.

"And the part that belongs to Koala," said Possum, who had been listening all the time. "If Koala helps, it's fair that Koala should have a part, too."

"But I CAN'T help," said Koala. "I have nowhere to put my gum leaves."

"I could store them for you," said Possum. "There is a store hole in my tree. You can store the gum leaves there. Then Cockatoo can use your billycan to fetch sticks to put in the bottom of the hole that Wombat is digging around the log so that it will be firmly wedged and won't wobble when Emu stands on it to reach the box."

"Well, that sounds like a good idea," agreed Koala. "And then we can all have a part of what's in the box. Possum must have a part too, because Possum will be helping."

"No, no, no!" spluttered Emu. "That's MY box, and what's in it belongs to me."

"Except for the part that belongs to me," said Goanna.

"And the part that belongs to me," added Wombat.

"And the part that belongs to me," screeched Cockatoo.

"And the part that belongs to Possum and me," said Koala.

"Oh, all right," mumbled Emu. "If you all help me, you can all have a part of it."

And so they all set to work. They put Koala's gum leaves into Possum's store hole. Cockatoo brought sticks in the billycan and laid them in the bottom of the hole that Wombat was digging, to wedge the log firmly so that it would not wobble when Emu stood on it to reach the box. And when Emu finally got hold of the box string, all the animals cheered. Now they would get their share of what was in the box. But Emu had other ideas. Emu seized the string and would not let go.

The other animals were not at all pleased with Emu. They started arguing and shouting and bumping into each other and bumping into Emu, who fell over and dropped the box!

And right away, the box bounced on the ground and burst open. All the animals rushed forward to claim their share of . . .

. . . NOTHING!

That wonderful box that they had all been struggling for was completely empty! It had nothing in it at all!

Which only goes to show that

IT IS VERY FOOLISH TO MAKE A GREAT BIG FUSS AND GET ALL WORKED UP OVER NOTHING AT ALL.

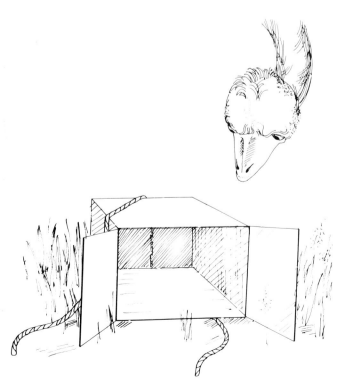

The Publisher, Author and Photographer acknowledge with thanks the facilities and assistance provided by the Sir Colin MacKenzie Fauna Park, Healesville, Victoria.

© Esta de Fossard 1984
First published 1984 by
Edward Arnold (Australia) Pty Ltd
80 Waverley Road
Caulfield East, Victoria 3145

Edward Arnold (Publishers) Ltd
41 Bedford Square
London WC1B 3DQ

300 North Charles Street
Baltimore MD 21201 USA

National Library of Australia
Cataloguing-in-publication data
De Fossard, Esta, 1934–
    Koala and emu and the unexpected box.
    For children.
    ISBN 0 7131 8097 8
    ISBN 0 7131 8098 6 (kit of book and cassette)
    I. McLeod, Neil. II. Twelftree, Lynn. III. Title.
A823'.3

Photography: Neil McLeod
Drawings & Book Design: Stott & Twelftree, Melbourne
Set in Garamond by Meredith Trade Lino Pty Ltd, Melbourne
Printed by Tien Wah Press